Christian

The Care and Feeding of a Grinch

A Random House PICTUREBACK® Shape Book

by Max the Dog, as told to Bonnie Worth • illustrated by Christopher Moroney

Based on the motion picture screenplay by Jeffrey Price & Peter S. Seaman.

Based on the book by Dr. Seuss.

Random House New York

www.universalstudios.com www.randomhouse.com/seussville

Published in the United States by Random House, Inc., New York, and simultaneously in Canada by Random House of Canada Limited, Toronto.

Library of Congress Cataloging-in-Publication Data
Worth, Bonnie.
The care and feeding of a Grinch / by Max the dog, as told to Bonnie Worth ; illustrated by Christopher Moroney. p. cm. — (A Random House pictureback) Based on the book, How the Grinch stole Christmas!, by Dr. Seuss. SUMMARY: Max the dog describes what his master, the Grinch, does when Christmas comes again to Whoville. ISBN 0-375-81021-8 (pbk.) [1. Christmas—Fiction. 2. Dogs—Fiction. 3. Stories in rhyme.] I. Moroney, Christopher, ill. II. Title. III. Series. PZ8.3.W896 Car 2000 [E]—dc21 00-21392
Printed in the United States of America October 2000 10 9 8 7 6 5 4 3 2 1
PICTUREBACK, RANDOM HOUSE, and the Random House colophon are registered trademarks of Random House, Inc.

I'm Max, I'm the dog, and my job is a cinch.
I keep a close eye on my master, the Grinch.
We look quite alike, if you see what I mean,
only my fur is brownish and his fur is green.

I know you are wondering, what does a Grinch eat?
A stinky raw onion is his kind of treat.
He likes food that's rotten. I guess you could say
the term for my master is Garbage Gourmet!

That's me, standing guard just outside of his cave.
I am scaring off Whos and I have to be brave.

Unlike all the Whos,
who like Christmas a lot,
my boss on the mountain
absolutely,
positively,
most assuredly
DOES NOT!!!!

Just where he went wrong,
I do not know at all.
It could be that his heart
is a wee bit too small.

He sneaks down to Whoville and likes to play pranks.
I have to help out, but he never says thanks.
One prank that we pull always works without fail.
We hide in the P.O. and mix up the mail.

A Who-gal named Cindy once fell down the chute.
I made the boss save her. (She *was* kind of cute.)

The gal missed the stamper by one little inch.
That day, Cindy Lou grew quite fond of the Grinch.
Like me, that gal knew that my master was good.
The Grinch was not evil, just misunderstood!

To honor the Grinch—give him reason to care—
was Cindy Lou Who's great idea of a dare.
And so Whobilation, which happens each year,
attempted to name him the chairman of cheer.

The boss was too shy. He did not want to come.
I used the old noggin and persuaded him some.
I helped him to dress and to clean up his face,
to come down and join in the whole Who-man race.

I’m sad to report he was not a success.

Too much food, too much noise, and
way,
way
too much stress.

Back up at the cave, as the boss sang a song,
he dreamed up a scheme—and I, Max, went along.
He put on a big suit of red trimmed with white.
He made me wear antlers. We waited for night.

We flew down to Whoville upon a great sleigh
and we made us some history that Christmas day.

He stole the Whos' Christmas—yes, lock, stock, and toy.
He unstuffed their stockings. (It gave him great joy.)
He came in the night like an evil green breeze
and he snatched all the wreaths and he swiped all the trees.

E·PLURIBUS·WHON

But the Whos fooled the Grinch in a wonderful way
as they all came awake on that Grinch-iful day.
And from up on Mt. Crumpit, we really could tell
that the spirit of Christmas was still live and well.

And then out of nowhere—well, what do you know?
His shriveled-up heart must have started to grow.
He gave them their Christmas, he brought it all back—
lock, stock, and toy—in a great bulging sack.

My boss now keeps Christmas alive in his heart,
and I like to think that I played a small part.
You have seen for yourself that it's really a cinch—
to give a dog hug to my master, the Grinch.